BABOONS!

Adapted by Apple Jordan
from the episode "Baboons!"
written by Kevin Hopps and Jack Monaco
for the series developed for television by Ford Riley

Illustrated by Francesco Legramandi and Gabriella Matta

A GOLDEN BOOK • NEW YORK

ISBN 978-0-7364-3563-5 (trade) — ISBN 978-0-7364-3564-2 (ebook)
Printed in the United States of America
10 9 8 7 6 5 4 3 2

It is early morning in the Pride Lands. Kion and the rest of the Lion Guard notice a group of vultures flying toward a baby baboon.

SCREECH! The baboon shrieks as he runs away in fear.

"Leave the baby baboon alone!" Kion roars up to the threatening vultures.

"Don't worry, baboonie!" cries Bunga, the honey badger, running after him as fast as he can. "The Lion Guard will save you!"

When one vulture dives toward the baboon, Ono swoops in, causing the mean bird to back off.

"Go ahead! Make your move!" the egret challenges. The Lion Guard has the vultures surrounded.

Mzingo, their leader, tells the vultures to give up. They fly away in defeat.

"You're safe now, little guy," Kion reassures the young baboon.

Fuli sighs. "Bothersome baboons and vultures. Could this day get any worse?" she says.

All of a sudden, there is a crack of thunder. The sky turns gray and rain begins to pour down.

The heavy rain quickly causes the river to flood. The shoreline where the baboon is standing is ripped away. The frightened baboon falls into the water and is swept down the river!

"Fuli, you have to save the baboon!" Kion orders. "You're the only one fast enough."

Fuli takes off at full speed and races along the shore.

The baboon reaches for a tree branch hanging over the river. He clutches it tightly until Fuli can help him.

"Hold on!" Fuli yells. She grabs the scared baboon by the scruff of his neck. "There," she says, pulling him to shore. "You're safe . . . again."

The baby baboon leaps up and gives Fuli a big hug. "Ugh," she groans. "Baboons!"

When the rest of the Guard catches up with Fuli,
they tell her that the river has washed away the strip of
land that leads to nearby Urembo Meadow. Now Kion's
sister, Kiara, and her friends are trapped on an island.
The Guard has to rescue them fast!

"You'll have to take the baboon home to Nyani Grove,"
Kion says to Fuli.

"Lucky me," she says, annoyed at the pesky baboon
still clinging to her neck.

Fuli races off to Nyani Grove.
She wants to get the baboon
home as quickly as possible.

"Hey! Come back here," Fuli says as the
playful baboon begins swinging from tree
branches. "Baboons!" Fuli chases after him.
"They never make things easy."

Meanwhile, the rest of the Guard goes to help Kiara, Tiifu, and Zuri.

Kion sees a big tree and has an idea. "We'll make a bridge!"

Beshte pushes with all his might against the large tree trunk. **CRAAACK!** The tree tips over and lands on the island. But the heavy tree causes the island's edge to crumble. It sinks into the rushing river.

Kiara gets nervous as she watches the raging river wash away small chunks of land. "We have to make a path to the shore ourselves," Kiara says. "All we need are a few big stones."

The three lions push a large boulder to the edge of the island. But the heavy rock rolls too fast. They can't keep up with it. **SPLASH!**

It falls into the river.

Ono tells the Guard that Kiara's plan didn't work. Kion gets an idea. "Maybe we can put our two plans together," he says. He asks Ono to fly back to Kiara, Tiifu, and Zuri. "Tell them to wait by the riverbank."

Bunga, Besthe, and Kion push a large boulder into the water. On the other side of the river, Kiara, Tiifu, and Zuri knock over a rotting tree. The tree cracks at its base and falls on top of the boulder, making a bridge. The plan works!

Kiara and her friends happily walk across to safety.

"We did it!" the Lion Guard cheers.

Farther inland, Fuli and the baboon have arrived at Nyani Grove. Several baboons pop their heads out from a tree to greet them. The leader thanks Fuli for making the long trip but tells her this is not the baby's home.

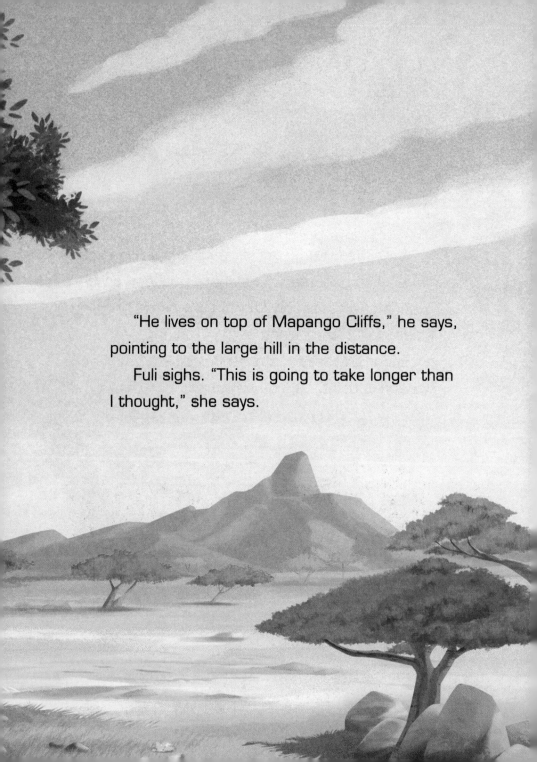

"He lives on top of Mapango Cliffs," he says, pointing to the large hill in the distance.

Fuli sighs. "This is going to take longer than I thought," she says.

Fuli runs even faster to reach Mapango Cliffs. Without the cheetah noticing, the baboon grabs a branch of a passing tree. He pulls himself up and hides high in the foliage.

Soon Fuli realizes something is different. The baboon is quiet. "A little too quiet," she thinks.

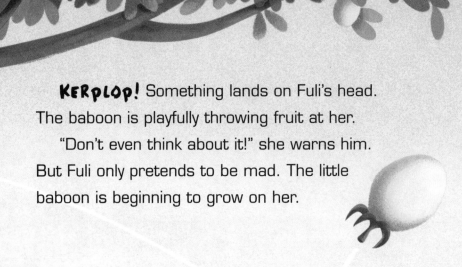

KERPLOP! Something lands on Fuli's head. The baboon is playfully throwing fruit at her.

"Don't even think about it!" she warns him. But Fuli only pretends to be mad. The little baboon is beginning to grow on her.

Fuli and the baboon finally make it to Mapango Cliffs.
"My baby!" the mother cries, hugging her little baboon.
"Guess my work here is done," Fuli says proudly.

When Fuli turns to head for home, she looks up in horror. The vultures are back—and they're flying straight for the baby baboon!

Fuli scrambles up the cliffs, while the baboons try to keep the vultures away by throwing fruit at them.

Fuli reaches the top of the cliffs. Then she leaps off and lands on Mzingo. They tumble to the ground. Fuli holds Mzingo down with her paws.

"Tell your birds to back off!" she demands.

Between the fruit-throwing baboons and tough Fuli, Mzingo knows he can't win. He orders the other vultures to leave.

As the vultures fly away, the baboons chant,
"Fuli! Fuli! Fuli!"

"Thank you for saving my baby," the mother
baboon says to her.

The baby baboon runs to give Fuli one last hug.
This time, Fuli smiles and happily hugs him back.

"Sorry I took so long," Fuli says when she finally catches up with her friends. "The baby baboon is home safe. It just wasn't as simple as I thought it would be."

"Bet you're glad to be rid of that baboonie," says Bunga.

"You know it," Fuli replies, but she can't hide her real feelings. She misses that pesky little baboon.